For Liz, who loves owls ~ C P

To my uncle Edvard Kristensen ~ T M

Copyright © 2008 by Good Books, Intercourse, PA 17534
International Standard Book Number: 978-1-56148-614-4

Library of Congress Catalog Card Number: 2007032363

Text copyright © Caroline Pitcher 2008
Illustrations copyright © Tina Macnaughton 2008
Original edition published in English by Little Tiger Press,
an imprint of Magi Publications, London, England, 2008.
Printed in China

Library of Congress Cataloging-in-Publication Data

Pitcher, Caroline.
The littlest owl / [text] Caroline Pitcher ; [illustrations] Tina Macnaughton.
p. cm.

Summary: Four, the youngest and smallest owlet of his brood, has a positive attitude
that gets him through most challenges of life in a nest, but it may not be enough
when a storm threatens his treetop home before he has learned to fly.

ISBN 978-1-56148-614-4 (hardcover)
[1. Owls--Fiction. 2. Birds--Infancy--Fiction. 3. Size--Fiction. 4. Self-esteem--Fiction.
5. Determination (Personality trait)--Fiction.]   I. Macnaughton, Tina, ill. II. Title.

PZ7.P6427Lit 2008

[E]--dc22

2007032363

The Littlest Owl

Caroline Pitcher   Tina Macnaughton

Intercourse, PA 17534
800/762-7171
www.GoodBooks.com

Deep inside a willow tree
were four white eggs.

One egg hatched,
then two, then three,
deep inside a willow tree.

Three owlets blinked at the last white egg.
One said, "It's very quiet in there."
Two said, "Maybe the baby can't get out."
Three said, "Maybe the egg is empty.
Maybe there isn't a baby inside."

"There is! Hoo-hooo, there's me,
there's me!" cried the last owlet,
struggling free.
　　And there sat Four, so dumpy
and small, a downy white ball.

Deep inside the willow tree, feeding time was such a scrabble. One, Two and Three snatched the food. They gobbled and gulped and blinked at Four.

One said, "Oh dear. He's dumpy."

Two said, "Oh dear. He's so small."

Three said, "He'll never grow big and strong like us."

"I will!" cried Four. "Just wait and see."

He scratched around in the bottom of the nest, and found a worm for his tea.

One, Two and Three grew more each day. They jostled and trampled Four, so dumpy and small, the downy white ball.

Mother Owl hooted, "Don't squash him, please!"

"I'm fine, Ma," he chirped. "I don't mind being small at all."

One, Two and Three were changing
fast. They shuffled out onto a branch.
They stretched their wings and
launched themselves into the air.
There they fluttered to and fro,
as soft as moths around the tree.
     Four called, "I'll fly too,
hoo-hooo, hoo-hooo."

Four hopped up and down along
the branch. He spread his short
wings wide and cried, "Wait for
me. I'm coming with you!"

But Four couldn't fly, however
hard he tried.

All night long
Four bobbed and bounced. All day long he fluttered
and flapped. "I will fly," he cried. "I will! I will!"
But he never even left the branch.
When dusk fell,
Four crept back inside
the tree and tumbled
into sleep.

Deep inside the willow tree the owlets
snuggled up and slept. But in the woods the
wind rose up. It gathered together a terrible
storm that whirled around the willow tree.
The tree was old. It groaned. It creaked.

"Wake up, wake up!" screeched
Mother Owl. "The willow tree will crack in two!"
    The sleepy owlets struggled out. One by one they
leapt and flew, and battled with the raging wind.
    "Come quickly, Four!" cried One.
    "What if he blows away?" cried Two.
    "What if he still can't fly?" cried Three.

The wind blew Four's downy feathers flat. It bounced him like a small white ball and tried to push him from the tree.

He stretched and strained, and flapped and cried, "I will do it too, hoo-hooo. Yes, I'm last and very small. But I'll never give up at all."

He hurled himself high into the air . . .

. . . and he flew
and flew
and flew!